First published in Great Britain by Hamish Hamilton Ltd 1984
Published by Simon and Schuster Books for Young Readers
A Division of Simon & Schuster Inc.
Simon & Schuster Building
Rockefeller Center
1230 Avenue of the Americas
New York, NY 10020

10 9 8 7 6 5

Simon and Schuster Books for Young Readers
is a trademark of Simon & Schuster Inc.
Printed in Belgium

Library of Congress Cataloging-in-Publication Data
Sadler, Marilyn.
Alistair in outer space.
Summary: When Alistair is kidnapped by a spaceship full of
Goots from Gootula, his main concern is for
his overdue library books.
[1. Science fiction.   2. Space flight—Fiction]
I. Bollen, Roger, ill.   II. Title.
PZ7.S1239A1   1988   [E]   88-6555
ISBN 0-671-66678-9

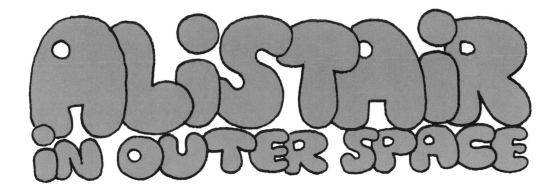

by Marilyn Sadler
illustrated by Roger Bollen

Simon and Schuster Books for Young Readers
Published by Simon & Schuster Inc., New York

Alistair Grittle was a sensible boy.

Every day he made a list of the things he had to do.
Then he made a list of the things he did not have to do.

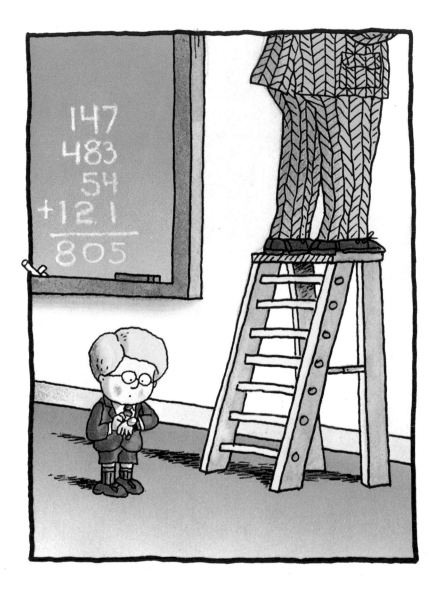

He was always on time for school. The school clock was set by Alistair's watch.

He hung up his jacket every night and put his shoes
in plastic bags.

Alistair took especially good care of library books.
He washed his hands before he read them so that he
would not smudge the pages. And he always returned
them to the library on time.

One day, when Alistair was returning his books to
the library, something unusual happened.

He was picked up by a space ship and whisked off into space.

Two creatures who called themselves Goots were flying the space ship. They were from a planet known as Gootula. They were very friendly.

The Goots liked Alistair very much and wanted to take
him home with them.

Alistair thanked the Goots very much. But he did not want to go to Gootula. "My library books are due back today," he said. "The librarian will be expecting me."

The Goots pretended not to hear Alistair and continued
on their way.

After a very short time, they landed on a planet they thought was Gootula. Then they realised that it was not Gootula. It was Trollabob.

"We must have made a wrong turn," said the Goots.

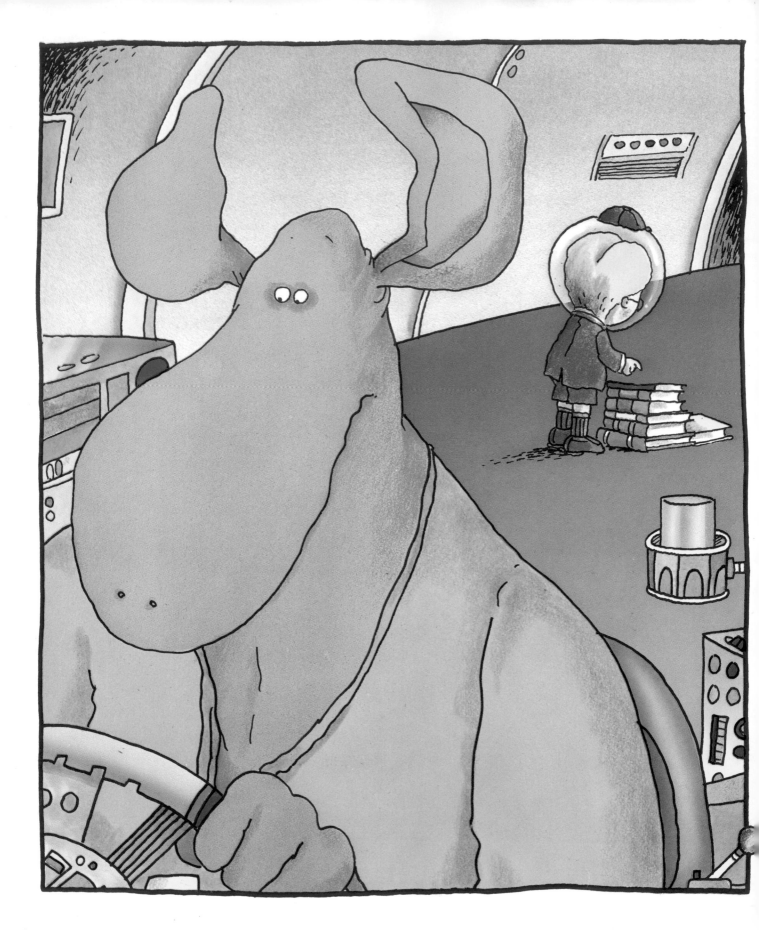

There was nothing for Alistair to do but read his library books again. Getting lost in an exciting adventure story was just what he needed.

But when he went to look for a place to wash his hands, he opened the wrong door. The next thing Alistair knew he was in outer space.

"Now I will never get my books back to the library,"
he said.

The Goots soon noticed that Alistair was missing, and they turned their ship around.

When they found Alistair, he was showing the Trollabobbles his library card.

The Trollabobbles wanted to take Alistair to Trollabob,
but he explained that he had just been there.

So the Trollabobbles gave Alistair back to the Goots.

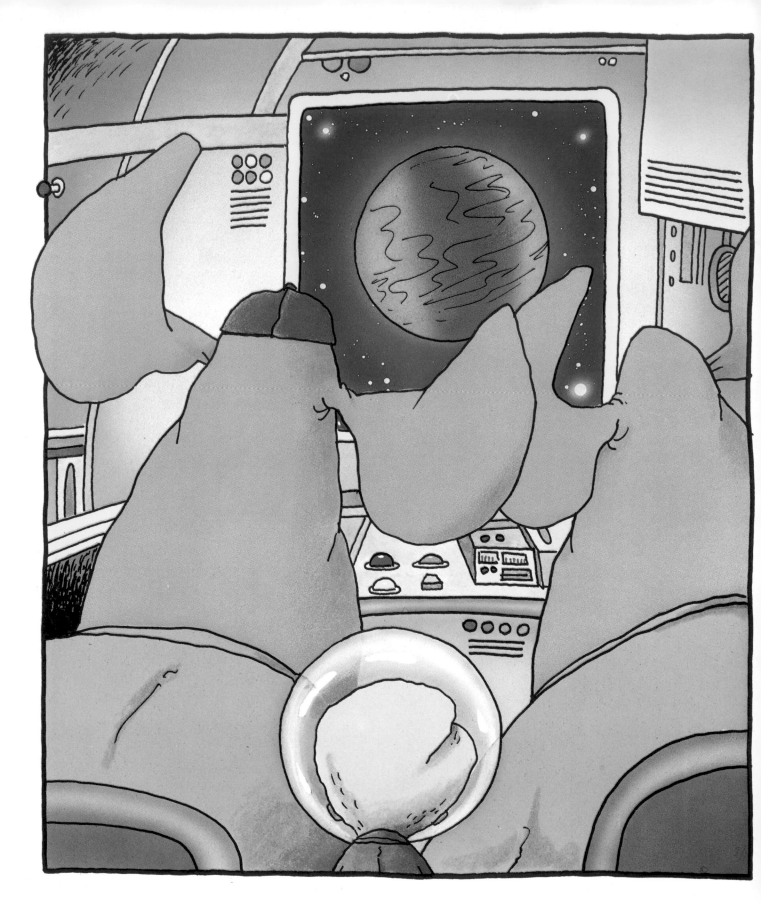

The Goots continued to search for Gootula, but they could not find it anywhere.

Alistair looked at his watch. It was getting late.
He was going to have to pay a library fine.

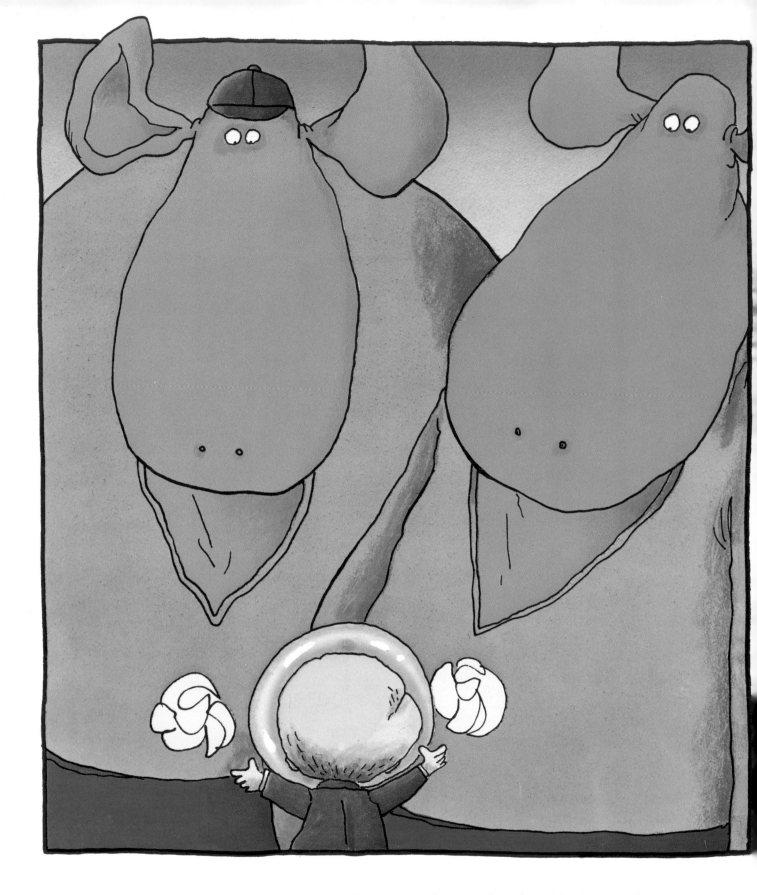

Alistair could not look for Gootula any longer. He insisted that the Goots take him home. This time the Goots agreed. They had never seen Alistair quite so upset.

The Goots told Alistair they were very sorry. Goots were not known to be good at directions.

Alistair did not think that the Goots would be able to
find Earth. So he decided to fly the space ship.

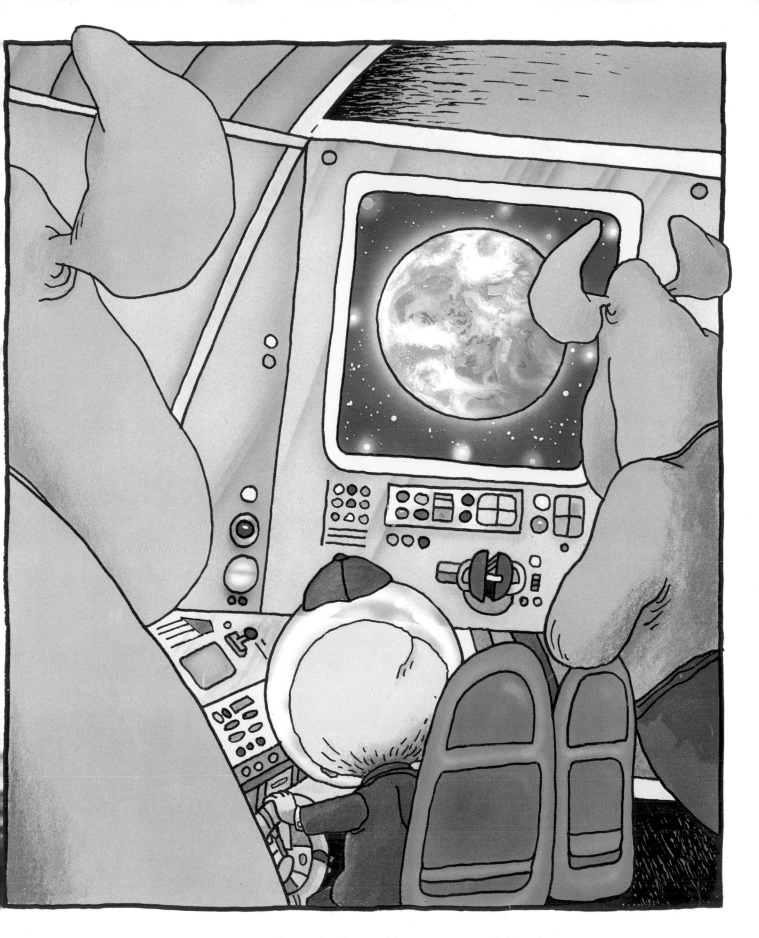

It was not very long before Alistair spotted Earth in the viewer. He was glad he had taken a shortcut.

Then Alistair let the Goots take over while he gathered up his books.

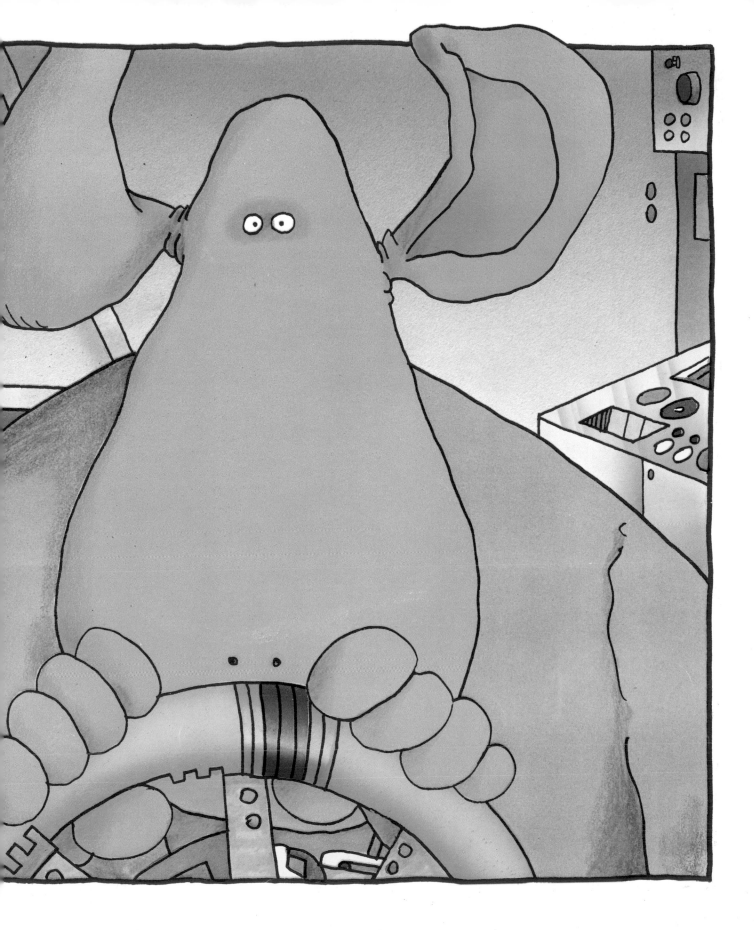

He was very much relieved when they finally landed on earth.

Although it was late, he was quite certain there would
still be time to get to the library . . .

. . . now that he was home.